# REBEL

By ALLAN BAILLIE ◉ *Illustrated by* DI WU

TICKNOR & FIELDS BOOKS FOR YOUNG READERS

NEW YORK · 1994

AUTHOR'S NOTE:

*Burma is known by two names. The military government calls it Myanmar,*
*but the Burmese still call it Burma.*

First American edition 1994 published by Ticknor & Fields Books for Young Readers
A Houghton Mifflin company, 215 Park Avenue South, New York, New York  10003.

First published in Australia by Ashton Scholastic Pty Limited

Manufactured in the United States of America
Typography by David Saylor
The text of this book is set in 19 pt. Garamond No. 3
The illustrations are watercolor and pencil, reproduced in full color

HOR   10   9   8   7   6   5   4   3   2   1

Library of Congress Cataloging-in-Publication Data
Baillie, Allan.
Rebel / by Allan Baillie ; illustrated by Di Wu — 1st American ed.   p.      cm.
Summary: When the General marches into Burma to take over,
one student is brave enough to rebel.
ISBN 0-395-69250-4
[1.  Courage––Fiction.  2.  War—Fiction.]   I.  Wu, Di, ill.   II.  Title.
PZ7.B156Re   1994
[E]—dc20      93-23512     CIP      AC

*In memory of Dr. Than Lwyn*

THE GENERAL came across the dusty
plain of Burma in the early morning.

He came with clanking tanks,
wheeled guns, and creaking trucks.

And long columns of crunching,
hard-faced soldiers.

They marched over the bridge,
past the ancient pagoda and the
quiet shops. They stopped
outside the schoolyard.

The General patted his hand with his baton
and looked at the school.
And the children inside the school looked
at the General.

The General pointed his baton, and the tanks rolled over the school's fence. The children watched the tanks flatten the slides, the swings, and the monkey bars.

Nobody spoke.

The hard-faced soldiers spread through the town,
kicking down doors and waving guns.
They brought every person before the General.

The General climbed onto a tank. He stroked his baton and
nodded. The gold stars on his hat flashed in the sun.
He rolled his shoulders so the rows of medals clinked
proudly on his chest.

He looked down at the townspeople and smiled at them.
They looked back at him but nobody smiled.

He said, "You are my people now. I have the tanks
and the soldiers, and you have nothing. I make all
the laws, punish who I wish, tell you when to
plant the rice and when to harvest it."

Nobody spoke.

"You will give me half of everything you make, and at school
the children will learn only of my heroic battles and
my glorious victories . . ."

At that moment, a small, battered thong was flung from the school building.

It whirled past three wide-eyed washerwomen,

flipped over a frightened fireman,

skimmed over a sleepy sergeant . . .

and hit the General behind the ear.

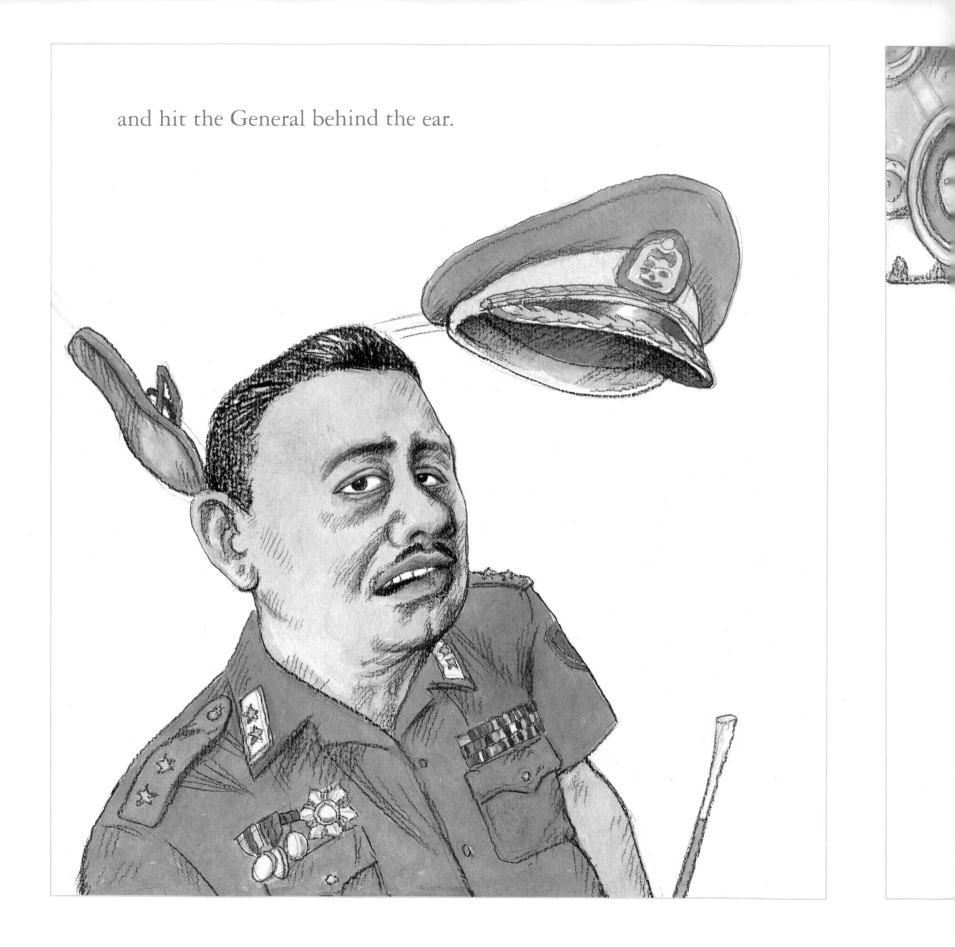

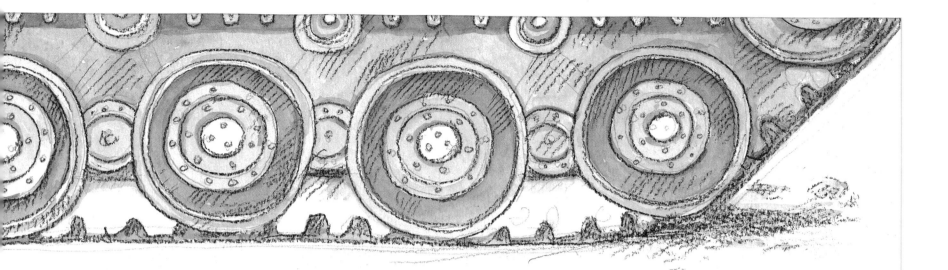

The General's hat dipped onto his nose,
bounced on the cannon of the tank,
and flopped into the dust.

Nobody moved. Nobody breathed.
Everybody waited through a long
and terrible silence.

The General stared down at his hat in the dust
and began to hiss.

"What!" he roared, and struck
his leg hard with the baton.

He turned slowly to the school, his medals clicking, his mustache twitching.

The sergeant darted forward, picking up the General's hat and the thong.

*"Who did that?"* bellowed the General.

There was no sound, no movement, from the school.

The sergeant furiously dusted the General's hat and polished the stars.

The General snatched his hat from the sergeant and rammed it on his head. "I will get the little rebel who attacked me and put him in a parrot's cage. And feed him on pig's swill. And . . ."

The General saw the thong in the sergeant's hands and plucked it away with his baton. "Ah hah!" he said.

"Bring all the children outside. Find the child wearing only one thong and drag him to me!"

The soldiers crunched into the school waving their guns,
and they lined up the children before the General.

They stood straight as posts, the children and their teachers,
and looked right past the General.
The General looked at the children and glared.

The hard-faced soldiers looked at the children and began to cough. Their hard faces began to twitch.

The townspeople looked at the children and smiled and grinned, and somewhere someone began to giggle.

The General stood on his tank,
tinkled his medals, shone his stars
—and broke his baton.

For in that school there was a large
pile of thongs, and all the children
and all the teachers had nothing—
nothing at all—on their feet.

The General went past the noisy shops,
past the ancient pagoda, and over
the bridge. He went with clanking tanks
and wheeled guns and creaking trucks.
And long columns of
marching—grinning—
soldiers.

The General marched across the
dusty plain of Burma in the late
afternoon.

But he could still hear the laughter.